WRITTEN BY G. M. BERROW

Contents

CHAPTER 1
Welcome, Spring-Sproing Springtime

It was a perfect day in Ponyville. The clouds had finally cleared and rays of sunshine illuminated every cottage, garden and cobblestone path. Ponies all over town emerged from their homes, blinking the sleepy winter out of their eyes. It had been almost a week since they'd finished their annual Winter Wrap-Up. They had spent an entire day clearing the paths of snow and ice, welcoming back their animal friends and ploughing the fields to get them ready for crops. Now every morning was like opening a present! The ponies loved being greeted by flowers and butterflies.

This morning, one pony in particular was feeling an extra spring in her step.

'Waaaaaaaaake up, citizens of Ponyville!' Pinkie Pie cried, throwing open her bedroom window on the top floor of Sugarcube Corner. No one was awake enough yet to hear her call out, 'It's going to be an awesome day!'

The candy-striped curtains rustled as a sweet, fresh breeze floated inside. Pinkie

inhaled deeply. 'Don't you just love spring, Gummy?' She bounced around her pet alligator with glee, her curly fuchsia mane puffing up.

Gummy blinked his large eyes in response, but his face remained blank.

'Smell this! It'll make you feel all flowery-powery!' Pinkie plucked a posy from her window box and bounded back over to him. The tiny gator opened his mouth, took the flower and swallowed.

'Ooooh, what a fun way to welcome spring, Gummy! Maybe I'll try it, too.'

Pinkie plucked another bloom and popped it into her mouth. 'Yuck! Maybe I'll stick to cupcakes for now.'

Pinkie trotted across the brightly coloured room. Everything in sight was patterned with hearts or balloons. 'So, what's on the PPP for today, Gummy?' She looked over her Pinkie Party Planner on the wall. It had been a gift from Twilight Sparkle and was where she kept track of all the exciting parties happening around Ponyville. Ever since she accidentally multiplied herself in the Mirror Pool in an attempt not to miss out on anything, she thought it was best to keep track of fun another way.

She scanned the list. 'Let's see . . . Ice-Cream Sundae Sunday party at Sweetcream Scoops's house? No, that's tomorrow. Silly me! Today is Saturday.'

She looked at Saturday – but there weren't any parties on today's schedule. Not one! Pinkie's jaw dropped, and she sunk to the floor. How could this be? A whole day with no fun activities to attend? What was she going to do?

Pinkie stood up straight with a determined look in her eye. 'There's no way we can waste such a prettiful sunshiny day doing nothing, Gummy!' She leaped over to a mountainous stack of coloured boxes in the corner – her party supplies – and started to riffle through them. Neon streamers flew through the air. Glitter confetti sprinkled down. Pointed party hats, noisemakers and birthday candles rolled across the floor. She was making a big mess, but she didn't care. She needed inspiration.

'Aha! This could be superiffic...'

Pinkie pulled out a shiny magenta cape edged in blue and yellow. She threw it over her shoulders and popped on a matching mask. 'A superpony party?'

Gummy blinked, unconvinced. Pinkie's shoulders sagged. He was right. The cape wasn't doing it. Pinkie tossed it onto the pile of rejected items and sighed. 'I know!' she said, brightening up again. 'How about a Capture the Flag tournament?'

Pinkie grunted as she struggled to push a massive gold box to the centre of the room. She placed a small ladder on the side and dived headfirst into the box.

Pinkie wasn't just looking for any old flag. She wanted a special flag, and she knew just the one. It was a keepsake from the time she'd been in charge of the flügelhorn booth at the Crystal Faire.

It had a sparkly pink flügelhorn on it. Sparkles were popular in Equestria – ever since the Crystal Empire had returned.

There were chequered racing flags, some Summer Sun Celebration flags, but no pink flügelhorn. Pinkie was out of luck. 'Oh well. Never mind!' she said. 'I'm sure there's something else ...'

Meanwhile, Gummy climbed on top of one of Pinkie's homemade Super Spring Sneakers – a set of shoes with giant silver springs attached to the bottoms for maximum bounce-ability. He slowly sprang up and down on one of them, and the shoe made a small squeaky noise.

'Gummy, you're brilliant!' Pinkie shouted.

She did a twirl that rustled up some stray confetti like a party tornado. 'Why didn't you say something?!' Pinkie strapped on her sneakers. 'We're going to have a Spring-Sproing-Spring Party to welcome the new season!' And with that, Pinkie bounced out of the door. It was time to get this party started!

CHAPTER 2
Pinkie's Party Ponies

Whenever Pinkie Pie went somewhere, she preferred to hop, skip or bounce rather than trot or walk. Today, with her spring-loaded sneakers strapped to her hooves, she was bouncing high into the sky. 'Hellooo!' she chirped as she poked her head through a cloud, surprising a green Pegasus with a yellow mane who had been asleep.

Boing! B-b-ba-doing! Boing! Within a few minutes, Pinkie found herself on the outskirts of Ponyville. 'Whoopsy-doodles! I overshot my bounce range again!' she giggled before heading back to where she had meant to land – right in the centre of town. It was the best spot to start telling everybody about the Spring-Sproing-Spring Party.

Pinkie looked out into the now-busy marketplace. She began to do a bubbly dance routine. 'It's spring! It's spring! What a wonderful thing! It's time to laugh; it's time to sing! But most of all . . . it's time to spriiiiiiiiing!' Pinkie Pie spread her hooves out wide and smiled. 'You're all invited to my Spring-Sproing-Spring Party! This afternoon! By the lake! Be there if you like having a little fun, a lot of fun, or even just medium fun!'

Sea Swirl and Rose trotted past, giggling and shaking their heads. They were used to seeing Pinkie act silly. Pinkie shrugged and started her song again. 'It's spring! It's spring! What a won—'

All of a sudden, a little voice interrupted her.

'Can we come, Pinkie?' said Apple Bloom in her cowgirl accent, jumping up like a baby lamb. She was a light yellow-green filly with a bold pink mane. She hadn't received her cutie mark yet. Her best friends, Scootaloo and Sweetie Belle – also 'blank flanks' – were with her.

'Of course!' Pinkie shouted. 'Everyone's invited! Especially you three!'

'Yay!' The three ponies erupted into a tizzy of excitement. Parties in Ponyville were common, but they weren't usually called out as guests of honour.

'Will there be bouncing?' asked Scootaloo.

'Will there be springing?' added Sweetie Belle.

'What about sproinging?' squealed Apple Bloom.

'All of them!' shouted Pinkie. 'And big trampolines, a bouncy barn and bungees! All of the springiest things there are.' She beamed proudly.

'Well, count the Cutie Mark Crusaders in,' said Apple Bloom. She turned to her two friends. 'Maybe one of us will get our cutie mark while we're there!'

'Yeah!' Scootaloo chimed in. 'My hidden talent could be . . . jumping?'

'Let's find out!' Pinkie pulled three sets of mini spring-loaded shoes just like hers seemingly out of nowhere.

'Wow, these are for us?' Apple Bloom put a pair on her hooves. She gave a little bounce and nearly lost her footing. It wasn't as easy as Pinkie made it look!

Pinkie's face grew serious. 'I need you to help me out. Everyone looks so busy, but I don't want them to miss this beautiful new spring day! Can you spread the word?'

'We'll do it!' the Cutie Mark Crusaders

said in unison.

'Awesome!' Pinkie replied with a jump. 'I've always wanted some Party-Planning Ponies!'

The three fillies puffed up with pride.

'OK.' Pinkie pointed to Sweetie Belle. 'Start by finding your sister. Go!'

Sweetie Belle bounced towards Rarity's home and shop, the Carousel Boutique. Rarity was probably there, working on some new outfits.

'Scootaloo, you head towards Rainbow Dash's cloud and tell her about the party, so she can tell everyone in Cloudsdale!'

'And you, Apple Bloom,' Pinkie said, looking down at the little filly, 'are in charge of rounding up the Apple family!'

'Aw, man,' said Apple Bloom, scuffing the dirt with her hoof. 'Can't I go somewhere other than my house?'

Pinkie cocked her head to one side, pondering this. Of course Apple Bloom didn't want to go to Sweet Apple Acres – she spent every day and night there! 'You're right, Apple Bloom,' Pinkie agreed. 'Why don't you take the path to Fluttershy's and stop at Twilight's library on the way?'

'I'm on it!' Apple Bloom was off.

Pinkie smiled. She was glad that her little Party Ponies understood how important the party was going to be.

CHAPTER 3
The Road Less Sparkled

Before heading to Sweet Apple Acres to invite Applejack, Pinkie decided to take a mini detour. She would stop by Cheerilee's house, Sweetie Drops's cottage and Cranky Doodle Donkey's place on the way.

As Pinkie Pie bounced up the path

to Cheerilee's house, humming a tune, she noticed something shiny on the ground. She bent down from her tall shoes to examine the mysterious glimmer. 'I spy with my little Pinkie Eye, something SHINY!' It was none other than a red ruby! Sunshine reflected off its facets, making it appear extra gorgeous.

'Wowza!' exclaimed Pinkie. 'Sparkly-warkly prettiness!' Getting excited over a ruby made her feel like Rarity, who had a talent for finding precious stones with her magic. Pinkie didn't have that, yet there was the little stone – just sitting on the path. But what was a ruby doing there? Maybe someone had dropped it! Pinkie looked around. There wasn't a soul in sight. 'Come with me!' Pinkie said to the stone. 'I'll help you find your owner!'

Pinkie tried to pick it up, but the ruby wouldn't budge. She pulled and twisted in every direction, but it remained stuck to the ground. Suddenly, she toppled hooves over head into a hedge. Her springy shoes had bounced her backwards!

Pinkie popped out of the bush and looked again. The ruby really was stuck to the path . . . but why? Just then, Pinkie noticed lots of other sparkles all around her. The path was dotted with colourful gemstones wedged between the normal grey, black and white rocks. They looked like rainbow sprinkles on a giant cupcake!

'Ooooh . . . ahhhh . . .' cooed Pinkie, her smile widening in delight. 'What a fun new way to spruce up a front garden.' She hopped from stone to stone, looking

down at the spectrum of precious gems. 'Hey there, Emerald! How's it going, Sapphire?'

Then, a mauve-coloured pony with a light pink mane and a cutie mark of three smiling daisies opened the door. 'Pinkie Pie!' she said. 'I thought I heard someone.'

'Hiya there, Cheerilee! I was just talking to your gems!' Pinkie bounced over. 'Your front path is like a party under your hooves!'

'Thanks, Pinkie! I just installed it. New garden gems from the Crystal

Empire. I didn't want to be one of those ponies who follow all the Canterlot trends, but this one is just so lovely.' Cheerilee was usually a no-frills sort of pony, but apparently even she couldn't resist some glitz and glamour.

'Abso-tootley-lutely!' Pinkie agreed.

'So, what brings you to my house this morning?' asked Cheerilee.

Pinkie smiled. 'Well, since you asked . . . do you like having a little fun, a lot of fun, or even medium fun?!'

Cheerilee considered the question. 'Well, I guess if you were twisting my hoof, I'd have to choose "a lot of fun".'

'Guhhh-reat!' Pinkie said. 'Because you're invited to my totally awesome Spring-Sproing-Spring Party! It's to welcome spring, and it's guaranteed to be any level of fun you want!'

'I'll be there,' Cheerilee laughed. 'What would Ponyville do without all your parties, Pinkie?'

Pinkie shuddered at the thought. 'It would probably be really, really boring!' she said. 'See ya later, Cheerilee! Bring friends! Bring bunnies! Bring bouncy things!'

As the excited pony took off, it was hard to tell which thing shone more – the pretty path or Pinkie Pie herself.

CHAPTER 4
The Spring-Sproing-Spring Party

'What in Equestria will Pinkie dream up next?' Twilight Sparkle said to Fluttershy. 'Look at this place!' The two pony friends stood on the sidelines of the Spring-Sproing-Spring Party, taking in the splendour and warm spring sunshine.

As Pinkie had promised, the area by the lake was decorated in a springy theme. Corkscrew streamers and ribbons hung from the trees. Three massive pink trampolines were set up, along with a bouncy barn, skipping ropes, a big bin of bungees and a bunny bed. It was the springiest place anybody had ever seen.

'I can't believe Pinkie Pie put all this together in just one day!' Fluttershy said in her soft voice.

'And Angel Bunny sure is having fun.' She pointed to where about twenty-five bunnies were hopping up and down on a mattress, giggling. Nearby, Rainbow Dash was taking her turn on a trampoline.

'Look at Rainbow over there,' added Applejack, trotting up and joining them. 'She sure knows how to put on a show!' Rainbow did a triple backflip, and everyone cheered.

'Totally cool, Rainbow!' squeaked Scootaloo. Rainbow Dash was her idol.

'Do it again!' shouted Lemon Hearts, a yellow unicorn with a sky-blue mane.

Rainbow didn't miss a beat. She shouted, 'You think that was cool? I have another trick that's at least forty per cent cooler!'

She launched herself into a triple-flip routine that would have shamed any circus pony. She jumped high into the sky, burst through a fluffy cloud and somersaulted back down to the trampoline – all without using her wings. The crowd roared.

'Wheeee!' Pinkie Pie bounced up to her friends, still wearing her shoes with the giant springs. 'Hey, girls! Isn't this party hoppin'?' She laughed. 'Get it? *Hoppin'!*'

'You could say that,' replied Applejack. 'I'm going to go for a jump on that bouncy barn. Looks almost like the one we have at home! Except it's inflatable.'

'Of course it does! I designed it based on the one at Sweet Apple Acres. You want to know why? Huh? Huh? Huh?!' Pinkie asked, nodding her head. 'Because he's the friendliest barn I know. You sure raised him well, Applejack!'

'I wasn't aware you knew a lot of barns personally, Pinkie,' Twilight joked.

It amused her that Pinkie was now making friends with buildings. What was next? Hanging out with vegetables? A picnic with trees?

'Oh, I *do*,' said Pinkie. She began talking fast. 'You'd be surprised! There's the rock farm barn, the barn at Nana Pinkie's, the barn at Granny Pie's – that one's a *little* grumpy – and a gazillion trillion more!' Her mane was puffed up to full height, which meant that Pinkie was very excited. Either that, or she'd just been jumping a lot. Or both. 'So, have you guys tried any of the super-fun activities yet?!'

Rarity, who had just joined them, sighed loudly. 'Oh, you know I would, darling, except I just can't stand the thought of having to fix my mane afterwards. Jumping and perfect hair do *not* go together!' She flicked her shiny purple coif and trotted off to go check out her reflection in the lake.

'Okeydokey-lokey!' Pinkie replied, unfazed. 'Catch ya later, Rarity!'

Twilight watched as Spike dived off the bungee platform, laughing as he sprang back up like a baby dragon-sized yo-yo. 'Well, Pinkie, I'd say your Spring-Sproing-Spring Party is a smashing success,' she said. 'It seems like every pony in town is here! Even some ponies I've never seen before. Like that group over there.' Twilight gestured towards the bouncy barn, where an older couple stood with their two daughters.

The old stallion had a light brown coat and grey mane with long sideburns and wore an old-fashioned hat and tie. His wife had a light grey coat and wore her dark grey mane tied up in a bun, along with glasses and a stern expression on her face. The two young mares were different shades of grey. Their manes were both bone-straight, but one of them had her fringe cut evenly across and the other had hers flipped over to one side. They were frowning at the festivities going on around them.

Twilight furrowed her brow, wondering why the family was acting so odd. 'Maybe they are new to Ponyville, or they are just passing through?' They seemed confused and lost. The two young ponies looked up at the large inflatable barn like they'd never seen one before.

'New ponies? Oh boy, oh boy! Where?!' shouted Pinkie, darting across the field. She loved nothing more than welcoming new residents to town and learning every single thing about them. A pony could never have too many friends! She ran back and forth, scanning the crowd until her eyes landed on the group. The smile on her face grew to maximum Pinkie happiness.

'I don't believe this!' Pinkie screamed with joy. She bounced up to the top of the bungee platform and pulled out a glittery pink megaphone. 'Fillies and gentlecolts! Your attention, puuuuh-lease!'

Everyone stopped jumping and turned to Pinkie for her big announcement. 'I'd like you all to welcome to Ponyville . . . my

FAMILY! Look! It's really them!' Pinkie threw confetti onto the crowd and a cheer rang out. 'That's my mum, Cloudy Quartz, and my dad, Igneous Rock! And my two sisters – Marble Pie and Limestone Pie!' The crowd craned their necks to get a better look.

'That's Pinkie family?' Spike said to Twilight. 'They don't look anything like her!'

'Maybe they are one of those families that are similar in other ways,' Twilight suggested. They did look a bit plain compared to Pinkie. But families came in all shapes, sizes and colours.

'Yaaaaaaay! Familyyyyyy!' Pinkie jumped onto a trampoline, using it as a launch pad to land in front of her sisters. She loved parties and she loved surprises... But a visit from her parents and sisters at one of her parties? That was the biggest surprise of all!

CHAPTER 5
Hard Times on Rock Farm

Her family all wore blank expressions as Pinkie twirled with glee. It was obvious that Igneous Rock had dealt with Pinkie's exhausting energy many times before. He stood patiently for a while, waiting for her to calm down. But soon he grew tired of the act. 'All right, now,' he said. 'That's enough.' But Pinkie was too excited to notice his disapproval.

Meanwhile, Twilight, Applejack, Fluttershy, Rainbow Dash and Rarity stood close by. They'd heard a lot about Pinkie's days growing up on the rock farm, but they'd never met Pinkie's family before. Some of the other party-going ponies started to gather round, too. They were also curious to learn more about the relations of the most popular pony in town. The chances were good that her family was totally fun, too.

'Hi, Mum! Hey there, Dad! How's it going, Marble? What's new, Limestone? Where's—?'

'Your older sister is keeping an eye on the farm,' Igneous cut her off.

'Oh, OK. What are you doing here?! I'm so totally surprised!' Pinkie skipped around them. 'Are you here to party? I planned all this! There are really cool—'

'Pinkamena Diane Pie,' Igneous interrupted. 'We are not here to party.'

Pinkie stopped still. 'You're not?'

'No,' Cloudy Quartz replied. Marble and Limestone shook their heads.

'Well, why did you come to a party, then, you bunch of silly heads? A party is the absolute *worst* place to *not* party!' A couple of ponies laughed.

'Pinkamena, don't you start with me . . .' Cloudy warned, looking down.

'Sorry,' Pinkie said, her mane deflating. 'I'm just excited to see you. It's been super long! You never usually leave the farm. Oh – is something wrong with Rockie?'

'Who's Rockie?' Cloudy asked.

'Rockie's my pet rock, Mum! He's grey, lumpy and about this big?' Pinkie motioned with her hooves. 'I definitely introduced you to him.'

'Oh,' replied Cloudy Quartz.

'Anyway, I only left him back at the farm because he said he'd miss all of his rock buddies,' Pinkie explained to her friends. She turned back to her parents. 'Marble and Limey promised to look after him!'

Marble Pie's face remained blank. Limestone Pie blinked.

Igneous cleared his throat and started to pace back and forth across the grass. 'This here has got nothin' to do with pet rocks or parties, Pinkamena.'

'Well . . . why are you guys in Ponyville, then, Dad? Huh? Huh? Huh?' Pinkie looked at the faces of her family but couldn't read them at all. 'Oooh, let me guess! Are we going on a family holiday to Appleloosa? Or... I know! I know! You came to bring me some of Granny Pie's scrumptious rock cakes! No, that's not it... OK, I give up! Tell meeeee!' Pinkie's eyes were practically popping out of her head with excitement.

'Your mother, sisters and I are here for a very important reason,' Igneous began. Pinkie frowned. Whatever it was, it didn't sound fun at all. It sounded... serious.

'Well, word got 'round that you are friends with—' Igneous looked around nervously, realising that he had an audience of curious Ponyville residents watching his every move. 'We heard that you might know...' Igneous puffed up his chest and finally announced, 'We are here to see Her Royal Highness, Princess Twilight Sparkle, regarding an urgent business matter!'

'We need to see the princess,' Cloudy said. The sisters nodded in unison.

Pinkie's face dropped. 'You're not here to party *or* to see me?'

'I'm sorry, but we have to talk to the princess and then get back to the farm right away,' Cloudy replied. 'We don't have time for any of this party nonsense.'

'Oh, I see,' Pinkie sighed.

'It's not nonsense!' Twilight said, stepping forward. 'And I'm right here.'

Everyone turned to look at Twilight, who up until now had been blending into the crowd. Usually she preferred that everyone treated her like they did before she became a princess. Twilight still wasn't used to all the attention, but she would do anything to help a friend, and it seemed like Pinkie needed her to play the princess role today.

Twilight spoke in her most regal voice. 'Welcome to our fair Ponyville.' She bowed.

Igneous, Cloudy, Marble and Limestone bowed their heads and leaned their front hooves on the grass to show their respect. 'Princess!' Igneous Rock said. 'Thank you for having us. We'd be so grateful if you'd help us out.'

'I'll help in any way that I can, Mr Rock,' Twilight said. 'Pinkie is, after all, one of my *very best friends*.' Cloudy and the sisters looked down at their hooves, embarrassed at how they'd just treated

Pinkie in front of royalty.

'That's great, Your Royal Highness,' said Igneous, taking off his hat. But he didn't sound too happy. 'It's great news . . . because we are about to lose the rock farm.'

'What?!' Pinkie Pie leaped into the air.

'How dreadful!' exclaimed Rarity.

'Oh no!' cried Rainbow Dash.

'Those poor little rocks,' Fluttershy whispered.

'Pinkie, are you OK?' asked Applejack, giving her friend a glance.

Pinkie's eyes were wide with terror, and she stood frozen to the spot. Fluttershy and Rarity looked concerned.

'Somebody poke her!' said Rarity. 'I've never seen her stand still before.'

Spike ran over and gave her a gentle nudge. 'Uhhh, you OK, Pinkie?'

Pinkie looked up, her face full of sadness. 'Everybody go home,' she said. 'This party is . . . over.' Everyone gasped. No one ever expected to hear Pinkie Pie say such a thing.

CHAPTER 6
The Pink Sheep of the Family

Pinkie Pie had always been the most fun-loving pony in town. If she was that upset over the closing of a rock farm, then it must be a big deal. For the rest of the day, Ponyville was abuzz with chatter about how Pinkie Pie herself had broken up a party! What was Equestria coming to?

'But I thought she didn't even *like* the rock farm!' Rarity whispered to Rainbow Dash. They were following Applejack as she led Pinkie's family over to the big barn at Sweet Apple Acres.

'Well, the rock farm was her home, so she's probably sad it will be gone,' Fluttershy said in her tiny, gentle voice. 'I can't imagine it.'

'Hey, are those emeralds around the flower border?' Rarity gasped, trotting up to the barn entrance. She was easily distracted by gemstones, no matter where they were. 'How *divine*!'

'Come in, y'all,' Applejack said, ushering her friends and Pinkie's family inside. 'We'll have a bit of privacy in here.'

She peeked her head out of the barn door to make sure there were no stray party ponies following them.

The Pie sisters looked at their surroundings in awe. Everything seemed to be so much brighter in

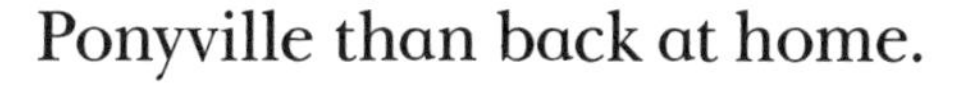

Ponyville than back at home.

'Good call, Applejack. Now, where were we?' Twilight walked over and hugged Pinkie. Luckily, she had perked up since Apple Bloom brought her an Emergency Cupcake.

'What happened to the farm, Mr Rock? And what can *all of us* here do to help?' Twilight wanted to make sure the family understood just how important her friends were to her. Being a princess required support. It wasn't just a one-pony job.

Igneous sat down on a wooden bench and hung his head. It looked as if he had the weight of the whole rock farm on his shoulders. Marble, Limestone and Cloudy Quartz trotted over and sat beside him. They all looked really sad.

'Go on now, Iggy,' Cloudy said. She patted her husband on the back. 'Tell the princess here what's going on.'

'Why don't you explain, Cloudy?' he said, looking tired.

'Yeah! Tell us, Mum!' Pinkie said, jumping up and down. She couldn't take the suspense any longer. 'Tell us now!'

But before she could begin, Limestone blurted out, 'It's the gems!'

'The gems?' Rarity asked. Any mention of jewels always piqued her interest. 'What about them?'

'Ever since that Crystal Empire showed

up again, all anyone wants are stones that shine, sparkle and shimmer!' Cloudy explained. Her bottom lip started to quiver. 'Plain old rocks are boring.'

'No, they're not, Mum!' Pinkie cut in. 'Rocks are awesome! There's slate! And granite! Marble! Mudstone! And—'

'Well, you tell that to the rest of Equestria,' Marble Pie replied. 'We haven't had any business for months!'

'That's awful!' said Twilight. She felt especially bad, thinking of all she had done for the Crystal Empire. She never expected the rest of Equestria to be affected by its return, especially by turning ponies out of their homes.

Pinkie suddenly recalled that very morning when she'd seen Cheerilee's gem-lined front path. And Rarity had just pointed out that the Apple family had put in some gems around the barn. It did seem like a lot of ponies in Ponyville were really into jewels lately. But Pinkie Pie never considered how that trend could be a problem for anyone.

Pinkie looked at the sad faces of her family. The gravity of the situation hit her like a ton of rocks. She had to do something to help them! Pinkie may have left her rock-farming days behind her, but the last thing she wanted was for her family to lose the farm. She pictured the old barn, the rock fields and the drab grey landscape. It wasn't much, but it was home. 'Thinkie, Pinkie!' she said to herself.

And then it came to her.

Pinkie began trotting around the barn, skipping and shouting. 'I know! I know!' She did a grand leap and landed right in front of her parents. 'We'll throw a party!'

'A party?' asked Cloudy Quartz. She furrowed her brow. 'I don't know...'

'Yeah! But not just any party, Mum!' Pinkie said, growing more excited by the second. 'A party dedicated to the total amazingness of rocks! It will be... a rock...a rock concert! We'll get bands and all sorts of rocks to decorate and invite every pony from every city all over Equestria to our very own ROCKIN' PONY PARTY!'

Twilight, Rainbow Dash, Applejack, Fluttershy and Rarity all turned to Pinkie's family for a reaction. Marble frowned. Limestone blinked. Cloudy winced.

Igneous remained stony-faced.

'What a splendid suggestion, Pinkie!' Rarity finally said, breaking the silence. 'What do you think, Mr Rock?'

'I think…' Igneous said, stepping forward. 'That it's…'

Everyone leaned forward. 'It's…'

Pinkie's smile grew with excitement.

'It's… the silliest idea I've ever heard in my life! This is not something one of your parties can fix. Why can't you be serious for once, Pinkamena?'

'I just thought it could be fun if—'

'Fun?' Igneous said. 'Why don't you run along now and leave us alone with the princess so we can figure this out for real?'

Marble flipped her straight grey fringe and nodded in agreement with her father.

Pinkie's face fell. She'd only wanted to help – in the best way she knew how. Ever since she'd left the rock farm, parties had been her life. Pinkie Pie loved nothing more than to make other ponies smile. A little fun could ease even the worst problems!

It had even worked the day Pinkie had got her cutie mark. She'd thrown her very first party for the whole Pie family, and they'd all laughed and danced and smiled! So why wasn't it working now?

Maybe they were right. Maybe she did need to stop being so silly. If it meant that much to her family, then it meant that much to her.

'Mum, Dad,' Pinkie Pie said, 'I, Pinkamena Diane Pie, *Pinkie Promise* to be a super-serious daughter from now on and not to throw any more parties! Cross my heart, hope to fly, stick a cupcake in my eye!'

Pinkie's friends looked at one another in shock. There was nothing that would make Pinkie Pie break a Pinkie Promise!

CHAPTER 7
Pinkamena Serious Pie

As soon as Pinkie Pie woke up the next morning, she went straight to work on becoming the new Pinkie she had promised to be.

'No more messing around, Gummy!' she said to her pet alligator. 'I'm Pinkamena Serious Pie now. Please don't bother me with any party invitations or cupcake offers. No swimming in the lake or dressing in silly costumes. All my time will now be devoted to finding a super-duper serious way to save the rock farm!'

Pinkie trotted over to the mirror next to her Pinkie Party Planner. Her reflection showed her hair had fallen a little flat against her head, almost as straight as Marble's and Limestone's. But she needed something else to look really serious.

Luckily, the mess she'd made the day before still covered the floor. There were flags, party horns and costumes all over the place. Pinkie spotted a great accessory for her new persona.

'These are perfect!' Pinkie snapped the fake nose and moustache off a pair of joke glasses and popped the frames onto her face. 'I look like I mean business.'

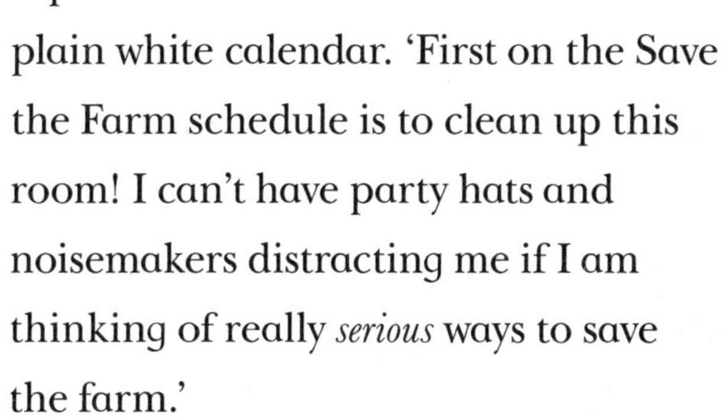

Pinkie ripped down the party planner and replaced it with a plain white calendar. 'First on the Save the Farm schedule is to clean up this room! I can't have party hats and noisemakers distracting me if I am thinking of really *serious* ways to save the farm.'

Pinkie got to work, packing up her party things. After she dragged the heavy boxes down the Sugarcube Corner stairs, she started painting her room a drab shade of brown. Then, she heard a hoof knocking on the door.

'Oooooh, a visitor!' Pinkie yelled out, forgetting to tone down her giddiness. 'I'll be there in two shakes of a little lambie's tail!'

Pinkie dropped the roller into the tray. It landed with a splat. Specks of paint splashed onto Gummy, who responded with his usual blink. Pinkie bounded to the door and flung it open.

Standing there was Twilight Sparkle. She was wearing her crown, which was odd because she usually didn't.

'Hellooooo, Twilight!' Pinkie sang out. 'I mean . . . welcome, Ms Sparkle. How may I help you?'

Twilight made a funny face. 'So you

were serious about being serious?'

'Abso-tootley-lutely!' chirped Pinkie, then quickly added in her new voice, 'I mean – yes, I am.'

'Why are you covered in chocolate, then?' Twilight asked, looking at the brown splotches all over Pinkie. Twilight didn't want to mention the odd glasses Pinkie was wearing. 'Were you baking your famous double chocolate chip "chipper" muffins?'

'No, silly-billy Twilight!' Pinkie Pie said. 'I'm redecorating! Or should I say… *undecorating*? Pinkamena Serious Pie would never have such a fun bedroom to play in. Once I do this, finding a way to save the farm will be a piece of rock cake!'

'Undecorating?' Twilight noticed the blotchy brown paint on the walls. What had Pinkie done? She loved her colourful room!

'Brown paint? No parties? Straight hair?' Twilight asked. 'Pinkie, this isn't you! We are going to plan the rock concert, just like you said! And we need your help.'

'Thanks, but no thanks, Twilight!' Pinkie shook her head. 'You heard them . . . My family isn't interested in my parties. I have to find another way to save the farm.'

Pinkie picked up the roller again and began to paint. Her glasses didn't fit and kept sliding down her nose. Whenever she pushed them back up, she smudged paint on her face. It looked funny, but Twilight couldn't even laugh. Her friend was in trouble!

Twilight trotted to the door, feeling defeated. 'Well, Pinkie, I guess it looks like *I'm* going to plan a rockin' pony rock concert. Let me know if you have any suggestions!'

Just maybe, if Twilight showed Pinkie how much the ponies needed her help with the party, she wouldn't be able to resist.

CHAPTER 8
Pinkie-less Party Planning

Twilight could already tell that Pinkie's family wasn't going to be much help, even though they'd finally agreed to let Twilight put on the show. When they'd heard it from the princess's mouth, it seemed like a better idea than it had when Pinkie said it. But it was too late – they'd hurt Pinkie's feelings, and now she was trying to be serious to please them.

'All right, everyone. Let's try to figure out how exactly Pinkie Pie does this,' Twilight Sparkle said. She was surrounded by books on rocks, party planning and music, but she had no idea where to start! Planning a rock concert was such a big task. 'Then we can figure out how to get Pinkie back to her normal silly self again.'

Twilight picked up a book called *Geodes of Western Equestria* and began to read aloud. ' "A geode is a spherical stone that has a plain, rock-like appearance on the outside but on the inside contains a glittering centre that—" '

Rainbow Dash and Applejack

exchanged a look.

'I'm sorry, Twi, but how is studying rock books going to help us plan a rock concert?' Rainbow Dash asked. 'Shouldn't we be out there getting our hooves dirty?'

'Maybe we should recruit some pony bands to perform,' offered Applejack.

'I could start on some decorations,' said Fluttershy. 'Or at least try to.'

Twilight closed the book. 'You ponies are right. This isn't getting us anywhere.'

'Where are the Pie sisters? Surely they have some ideas,' Rarity said. 'It is *their* party!'

'I doubt it,' answered Twilight, using her magic to put away the books. Her horn sparkled, and the hardbacks floated gently up to their shelves. 'If you haven't noticed, the Pies aren't too into parties. I only got them to agree to let us put on the concert by saying it was my official Royal Advice!'

'They looked so lost at the party yesterday,' said Fluttershy.

Twilight nodded. 'I completely agree. That's why Spike is giving them a tour of Ponyville. I told them that Spike was my Royal Tour Guide and it was a special honour to be shown around by him.'

'They sure do look up to ya, huh?' Applejack said. 'Bein' a princess and all!'

'Now if only they'd believe me when I say the best pony for this job is Pinkie Pie!' exclaimed Twilight. 'Then they'd see just how special she is to all of us.'

'Don't worry, Twi,' said Rainbow Dash. 'Once we start putting the party together,

Pinkie won't be able to help herself! I give her a few hours before she's in here, calling all the shots.'

Twilight looked down at her to-do list. 'Rainbow, you've given me an idea. I know how to get Pinkie back!'

CHAPTER 9
Perusing Ponyville

'And this is where we all go to buy our quills and sofas,' Spike told the visitors, standing in front of a little shop called Quills and Sofas. His presentation was met with little enthusiasm from Igneous Rock, who just stared back, chewing on a piece of hay.

'Is this where *the princess* buys her quills and sofas?' Cloudy Quartz asked. Marble and Limestone listened intently.

'Yes, Twilight gets all her quills from here, too ...' Spike groaned. Pinkie Pie's family certainly was starstruck by the idea of a royal pony in their midst. Every place they had visited, Cloudy had wanted to know Twilight's opinion on it. Marble and Limestone didn't say much; they just seemed to have an unspoken language that consisted mostly of blinks and nods.

'Does she send many letters to Princess Celestia? To Canterlot?' Igneous asked. 'I've never been there myself, but I hear it's very nice.'

'Well, actually, I send the letters,' Spike explained. 'She tells me what to write, and I put it on the scrolls!'

'Is that so?' Igneous eyed Spike

suspiciously. He still wasn't too used to hanging out with a talking baby dragon.

'I guess we can head to the Carousel Boutique next,' Spike announced, leading the way. 'Rarity owns it! She is known as the prettiest, um . . . I mean, most *fashionable* pony in town!' Spike still had a hard time containing his crush on Rarity. He blushed, but Pinkie Pie's family didn't even notice. They had their sights on something else.

All of a sudden, Marble and Limestone gasped. Cloudy yelled out, 'Iggy! Look at that over there!' They trotted over to Cheerilee's path and stared down at the glittering jewels.

'This is what's putting us out of business!' Cloudy cried. 'And I hate to admit it, but it *does* look nice.' She started to cry. 'We're doomed!'

Igneous hushed his wife. 'Calm down, dear. We've got a princess on our side now! She'll sort everything out. We'll all be back to work on the rock farm before you know it.'

Spike noticed Marble and Limestone Pie frown. They looked like they could use a little less work and a little more play. Maybe they could come and visit their sister again and learn about having fun. That is, if she ever went back to normal ...

'Oh, you're right, dear. Thank Celestia that Pinkamena is staying out of it like a good little filly,' said Cloudy. 'You know how that girl gets an idea in her head and won't let it go.'

'Mmmhmmm,' Igneous Rock agreed, tipping his hat.

Spike felt bad for Pinkie. The way her family treated her was ridiculous. She only wanted to help! And now she was driving herself bonkers trying to please them. The next stop on the tour had to be Sugarcube Corner. Maybe it would sweeten them up.

CHAPTER 10
A Visit to Sugarcube Corner

Pinkie had just finished changing all her bedroom accessories from bright colours to shades of brown and grey when she heard someone outside. She trotted over to the window. Down below, she spied her family! They were with Spike.

'Hey, parents! Up heeeeere!' Pinkie was excited to show them how serious she could be. 'Look up here!'

Finally, they saw their daughter. With her stick-straight mane and her glasses, she was looking more like them again.

'Pinkamena! What are you doing up there?' Igneous shouted.

'This is where I live, family! Come up!' Pinkie shouted. She turned to Gummy. 'Oh goody, goody rock hops! This is going to be fun! I mean – serious fun.'

A moment later, Igneous, Cloudy and Spike trotted into the room. Pinkie did a twirl. 'I *undecorated*! Just for you! Now I can be serious all the time!' Pinkie made a stern face. It didn't suit her.

'That's nice, dear. You've made it look

more like the barn back home. Is that Granny Pie's quilt?' Igneous pointed to the blanket on the bed – a grey-and-black creation with quilted rock shapes.

'Oh yes,' said Pinkie. 'That's my basalt blankie, all right! Where are Marble and Limey? I want them to meet Gummy!'

'They are waiting downstairs, Pinkamena,' her dad said, heading towards the door. 'We don't have all day to just chat! We have business with the princess.'

'Wait! You guys don't even want to hear my serious ideas to save the farm?' Pinkie said, looking crushed.

Cloudy patted Pinkie on the back before trotting out after her husband. 'That's nice, dear. Tell us later on.' Pinkie's shoulders slumped. Once again, she had been unable to please her parents.

'Bye, Mum. Bye, Dad,' she called out.

'Are you all right, Pinkie?' Spike asked, now very concerned. 'Are you sure you don't want to help Twilight and the girls with the party?'

There was a little glint in her eye, but it quickly passed. 'I'm totally fine-eriffic, Spike. I'll just have to try harder! No parties! Pinkie never breaks a Pinkie Promise, remember? See ya later!' Pinkie bounced out of the door.

'That's what I was afraid of,' Spike said

to Gummy. 'We've got to do something! Want to come and find Twilight?'

The little alligator blinked.

'I'll take that as a yes!'

CHAPTER 11
The Pinkie Trap

Rainbow Dash and Applejack stood in the road by Sugarcube Corner, waiting for Pinkie Pie to leave her house. 'Are you sure this is going to work?' asked Applejack. She looked up at the big bunch of balloons she was holding in her hoof. They looked pitiful. Every single one was misshapen or needed more helium.

'Are you kidding? Of course it will!' said Rainbow. 'Look at these! There's no way Pinkie will be able to stand how these balloons look. She'll want to show us how it's done. Then, she'll be reminded of how much she wants to help with the party and everything will be back to normal!'

'If you say so,' Applejack said, craning her neck. They'd been standing there for quite a while. 'I just hope we haven't missed her already.'

'Missed who?' asked Pinkie Pie, who had somehow appeared right beside them. 'Are you giving someone a balloon surprise?' Pinkie asked, eyeing the balloons hungrily.

'Well, not exactly…' Rainbow Dash said, playing along. 'See…Applejack and

I were just put in charge of balloons for the Rockin' Pony Party. How do these look, Pinkie? Perfect... *right*?'

'Yeah, they're, um...' Pinkie started to sweat, and her eyes began to dart around. She looked at the balloons, desperate to say something. Even her hair started to puff up a little teensy bit. 'They look just...'

'Yeah?' said Applejack. 'How do they look?'

'They look guh-reat! Keep up the good work!' Pinkie said, regaining her focus.

'No time to chat! Serious business to take care of!'

Rainbow Dash and Applejack sunk down in defeat.

'Bye, Pinkie!' Rainbow called out, and then turned to Applejack. 'I thought we had her for sure!'

'Don't worry. The others are ready to go,' Applejack reminded her, watching Pinkie canter off into the distance.

As soon as Pinkie turned the corner by the Carousel Boutique, Rarity trotted outside. 'Darling, I'm so glad I saw you passing by! I need your advice on these posters for the rock concert!' She pulled out a large stack of handmade posters, covered in

pictures of flowers and bows.

Pinkie scrunched up her nose. 'They're nice, Rarity, but why the flowers and bows? It's a rock concert, silly!'

Rarity smiled. 'Oh? Then what should I put on them?'

'Um . . . rock things?' Pinkie was using all her Pinkie Power not to explode into some sort of party monster right there. She was itching to take over, but she held fast to her promise to her family. 'Actually, I think they are great just like that. Good luck with the posters, Rarity! See ya!'

Rarity sighed as she watched her friend leave. 'Well, I *tried*,' she said to herself. 'These posters are absolutely hideous!'

But Pinkie Pie was on a mission. She *needed* to get to the library. Little did

Pinkie know, Twilight and some other guests were expecting her there, too.

CHAPTER 12
A Peace of Pie

As Pinkie made her way to Twilight's home at the Golden Oak Library, she thought about how she'd resisted helping Rainbow and Applejack with those poorly inflated balloons. And then she'd stopped herself from redesigning Rarity's posters, even though they'd made no sense. While she couldn't believe her own

Pinkie Power, she felt peculiar. Why had she given up parties again? Pinkie was starting to forget the reason.

'Focus, Pinkie!' she thought as the library came into view. 'You have to save the farm!' All she needed was a couple of books, and Twilight had to have them.

'Knock, knock, Twilight!' Pinkie shouted into the window. 'I really, really, really, really need some books!'

'Come in, Pinkie!' Twilight shouted out. 'What are you looking for?'

'Well, I'd like one on growing cucumbers and then one on how to run a rock circus and maybe a—' Pinkie pushed open the door, expecting to see Twilight and Spike. Instead, she saw them – plus Rarity, Applejack, Rainbow Dash, Fluttershy *and* Pinkie's whole family!

'Is this a surprise party?' Pinkie asked,

her glasses sliding down her nose. 'Because I'm tooootally surprised!' She started to smile, then looked at her family and remembered why she had come there in the first place. 'I mean, not that I like parties. Parties are the worst thing ever!'

'You know that's not true, Pinkie Pie,' said Twilight.

'Of course it is! I'm Pinkamena Serious Pie – the most serious-est pony in all of Ponyville. Maybe even Equestria! Would anyone like to schedule a business meeting with me?'

Pinkie pulled out a planner and pen and started scribbling furiously in it.

'No, but we would like our old friend Pinkie back,' Applejack said. Rarity, Fluttershy and Rainbow nodded.

'And we'd like our Pinkamena back, too,' Igneous Rock said, joining them. He looked embarrassed, but he was smiling.

'You . . . you would?' Pinkie couldn't believe her ears. 'But I thought . . . I thought you wanted me to be serious!'

'We're so sorry, dear,' Cloudy Quartz said. 'We didn't mean to hurt your feelings. We've just been under so much stress about losing the farm and, well . . . we didn't think you'd understand!'

'But I do understand!' Pinkie took off her glasses. 'I only wanted to help!'

'We see that, thanks to Princess Twi— thanks to all your *friends*,' said Igneous. 'You're a real lucky pony. They told us how you'd changed yourself just to please us. This talking baby dragon here was concerned.' Spike puffed out his chest.

'We didn't realise what we had done until we saw you out of the window just now, struggling to hold back your natural talent and not helping your friends.'

Cloudy shook her head. 'You don't need to do that ever again, Pinkie! We love you just as you are.'

'Oh, and I love you!' Pinkie ran over to her family and scooped up all four of them in a big hug. 'You guys are the bestie-westest!' When she pulled away, her mane was at maximum poof again!

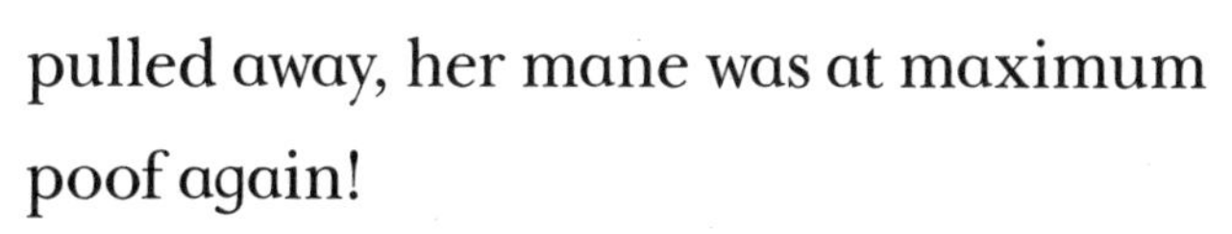

'Now we just have one question for you, Pinkie...' her mum said.

'What is it?!' Pinkie bounced up and down. 'Ask me! Ask me! Ask meeee!'

Igneous Rock cleared his throat. 'Will you plan our rock concert party?'

Pinkie pretended to think about it. 'Oh, all right. If you really want me to!'

Everyone cheered. Now they were really back in business.

CHAPTER 13
Pinkie Takes Action!

It was all hooves on deck to rescue the party, and Pinkie could not have been happier. She bounced about, speaking a million words a minute. Her family stood by, amazed.

'Rainbow Dash, you're in charge of invitations! I'll need hundreds of tiny bags of rock sweets with tiny parachutes on them! You can talk to Mrs Cake about the sweets and to Davenport at Quills and Sofas for the parachutes. Did you know he also does custom printing?! Little-known secret. You and the other Pegasi take them all over Equestria! GO!'

Pinkie's mane was getting fluffier with each second. 'Fluttershy, call Photo Finish and tell her to bring in some of her famous friends! We need the biggest and rockingest bands in all of Equestria to perform! I want every musician we know on that stage – Octavia! Lyra Heartstrings! DJ Pon-3! Lyrica Lilac! Neigh-Z! Don't worry. I have some secret connections if those ponies fall through!'

Pinkie winked at Twilight, who just looked baffled. No one knew that Pinkie had celebrity friends.

'Got it,' Fluttershy said softly.

'Applejack! Mum!' Pinkie shouted. 'You're next!'

'Me?' said Cloudy Quartz, looking around as if there were some sort of mix-up.

'Totally!' Pinkie laughed. 'You guys are in charge of TREATS! I want apples. I want rock cakes. Apple rock cakes! Enough to feed all of Equestria! Go, go, go!'

Applejack saluted Pinkie and led a very confused Cloudy out of the cottage. 'Come on, Mrs Quartz! We can go on a baking spree at Sweet Apple Acres!'

'Rarity! Twilight! Marble Pie! Limestone Pie!' Pinkie called out. 'You are in charge of...

DECORATIONS!' Marble and Limestone exchanged an excited smile, finally allowing themselves a little fun.

'Oooh! Just the job I wanted!' Rarity said, clapping her hooves together. 'OK, girls, I have some ideas for the main stage curtains! I'm thinking velvet, maybe grey satin? Black, shiny ropes and marble columns? Going with sort of a rock-stone-chic look?'

'That sounds amaaaaaazing!' Pinkie squealed. 'The more rocks, the better!'

'Got it, Pinkie!' said Twilight.

There was only one pony left without an assignment. Igneous Rock shuffled his hooves. 'What should I do, Pinkamena?'

'Dad!' Pinkie bounced over to him.

'You have the most important job of all!'

'I do?' he said. 'What is it?'

Pinkie jumped into the air. 'Have fun, of course!' she yelled before trotting out of the door. 'This totally rocks!'

CHAPTER 14
Pinkie Pie in the Sky

The roads to Ponyville were jammed with ponies from all over Equestria making their way to the concert. The skies were busy with Pegasus traffic, and the Friendship Express train was full.

Pinkie watched in awe from up in the sky. She was in Twilight's hot-air balloon, sprinkling the sea of ponies with rock-shaped confetti. 'Welcome to the ROCKIN' PONY PARTY!' she yelled into her megaphone. This was the biggest party she'd ever planned!

'Yaaay, rockin'!' Fluttershy yelled quietly, flying beside Pinkie. She landed inside the basket of the balloon and turned to Pinkie. 'You ready for your big entrance?'

They had it all planned out. Pinkie would land onstage, thank the guests for coming, and tell them about the rock farm. Then everyone would rock the night away!

'You betcha-wetcha, Fluttershy!' Pinkie yelled into her megaphone. It was so loud that it caused Fluttershy's hair to blow backwards in a gust of wind.

'Whoopsies!' Pinkie giggled. 'Sorry!'

'It's OK!' Fluttershy said, taking off. 'I'll see you down there soon, Pinkie!'

Moments later, Fluttershy arrived at the front entrance. It was decorated with several large rock piles, bunches of rock-shaped balloons and a banner. Twilight and the others were there, wearing their access-all-areas badges. Pinkie Pie's family stood beside them, watching the hordes arrive. There was a buzz in the air, and it wasn't just the happy bees that were flitting around in the fragrant flowers.

'This is sweet!' a tall royal-blue stallion yelled to his pack of buddies. 'I can't believe Pinkie Pie got Coldhay to perform! They are totally my favourite band of all time!'

'Yeah, and I heard they are going to do a set with the Whooves,' said his red stallion friend with a guitar cutie mark. 'It will go down in Equestria history!'

Igneous Rock's eyes were wide with disbelief. 'How did our little Pinkamena do all this?'

Cloudy's jaw was nearly on the ground. 'And they all came out to help us?'

'What did I tell you?' Twilight smiled. 'You have a very special daughter. She knows how to bring ponies together.' Twilight whispered

to Rarity, 'Let's hope it works!'

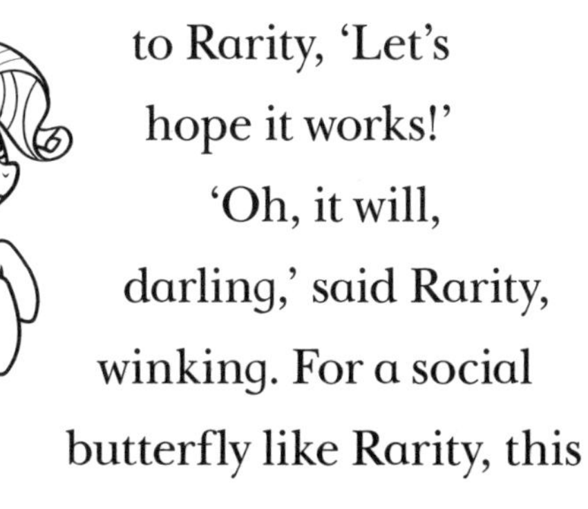

'Oh, it will, darling,' said Rarity, winking. For a social butterfly like Rarity, this was heaven. The two ponies hoof-bumped and ran off to their places. It was time to get this rock party started!

CHAPTER 15
The Rockin' Pony Party!

Inside the entrance, Applejack was working on the apple juice and rock cake booth. 'Come get 'em! Apple rock cakes! Pie family secret recipe!' she shouted to the crowds. She didn't need to try very hard to sell them. Cloudy Quartz had helped her with the recipe, and the cakes were delicious. The concertgoers were buying them faster than Applejack could serve them! They'd already sold two whole batches, and the show hadn't even started yet! 'Giddyup, Apple Bloom! Bring out another batch!'

'Got it, sis!' the little filly replied with an excited smile. Sweetie Belle and Scootaloo followed her. 'We'll help, too!'

Near the stage, Rainbow Dash was pumping up the crowd with some awesome Wonderbolt-style tricks. She dived into a barrel roll and flew right above the

hundreds of ponies. Then she landed on the stage and hoof-bumped a white pony with a blue-streaked mane and sunglasses. It was none other than DJ Pon-3, who was busy spinning some beats to get the party started on her turntable.

Suddenly, a couple of Coldhay's road-ponies burst through the crowd and ran towards the stage. Whispers of excitement rippled through the crowd, and everyone stamped their hooves.

The sun was starting to set over Ponyville as Pinkie Pie's balloon floated down onto the stage. DJ Pon-3 switched to a new song as Pinkie hopped out of the basket.

'Fillies and gentlecolts of Equestria!' she shouted into her megaphone. 'I'm here to welcome you to . . . the first annual Pinkie Pie Family Rock Farm Rockin' Pony Party!' The ponies went wild. Pinkie bounced and flipped all over the stage. 'Let me ask you this: do you love rocks?! I know I do!' she screamed into the megaphone. The crowd started chanting *rock*. 'Wahooo! Are you ready to rock?!'

'Yeah!' the crowd yelled back.

'All right! Please welcome Canterlot's very own . . . COLDHAY!!!' Pinkie Pie welcomed the band and waved to the crowd as she exited.

By the end of the night, it was Pinkie's

name that the ponies were all chanting. It was the most fun she'd ever had – because she was being herself and no one else. It rocked.

CHAPTER 16
A Rockin' Success

Over the next few days, all anyone could talk about was the success of the Rockin' Pony Party. The performances had been stellar; the ponies had danced all night. And most importantly, they were reminded of how awesome rocks were!

It was incredible how the rock farm

had gone from struggling to thriving overnight. Igneous and Cloudy were taking orders for garden-path stones, cottage bricks and even pet rocks!

When it was time for them to go home, Pinkie and her friends gathered to say goodbye. 'How can we ever thank you?' Igneous Rock said to his daughter. 'You saved the farm!'

'I could never have done it without the help of my friends . . . and you guys!' Pinkie giggled. 'Wasn't it a fantilly-astically great time?!'

'Abso-tootley-lutely!' said her dad with a wink. 'Come and visit us, now! Your mother's birthday is coming up soon.'

'A birthday?!' Pinkie's eyes grew wide.

'You know what that calls for?'

'A party!!' everyone chorused.

'Hey! How'd you guys know what I was going to say?!' said Pinkie Pie.

Read on for a sneak peek of the next exciting MY LITTLE PONY adventure,

Applejack and the Secret Diary

'Thirty seconds left, y'all!' Applejack hollered into a megaphone. 'Better hurry up an' eat yer treats!' At the sound of her voice, the contestants of the pie-eating contest all pushed harder to finish their pies. Pinkie Pie squealed gleefully and shoved another piece into her mouth with ease. A glob of sauce dripped onto her bib, which read PIE IS MY NAME. Next to her, little Scootaloo attempted in vain to munch on a second piece. She stopped mid-bite, held her tummy, and groaned. Minty and Lyra were in a similar state, only each halfway through a pie. But down at the end of the row, something interesting was happening.

Applejack couldn't believe her eyes. The clock had only twenty-five seconds left on it, but the most unlikely pony of all – well, technically he was a *donkey* – was in the lead to win the Seventh Annual Sweet Apple Acres Pie-Eatin' Extravaganza! Cranky Doodle Donkey usually liked to spend his days inside his cottage on the outskirts of Ponyville, minding his own business. But something about eatin' these pies must've cranked his gears, because there he was, shovelling them into his gob with the best of them.

'You can do it, Lyra!' shouted Sweetie Drops from the audience. She waved a homemade flag sewn with a picture of Lyra's cutie mark – a golden lyre. Lyra smiled and waved back, mouth full. The two ponies were best buddies.

Next in line was Mayor Mare. She was usually one of the most proper ponies in town. She was an authority figure, so she liked to remain composed. But right now, she was attempting to hold her own against Cranky. Her approach was unique. She took methodical, dainty bites and wiped her mouth after each one. She kept saying things like 'Oh my!' and 'Delicious!' and 'I couldn't possibly!'

The seconds ticked down on the timer. Everypony leaned in. It was now pretty much a race between Pinkie Pie, Mayor Mare, and Cranky Doodle Donkey. Minty, Lyra, and Scootaloo gave up and started cheering along with the crowd.

'Ten! Nine! Eight!' the ponies shouted. 'Seven! Six! Five!' Applejack trotted over to the three finalists. Pinkie Pie stopped and let out a loud burp, then giggled. The race was now between Cranky and the mayor. 'Four! Three! Two!' All of a sudden, Cranky grunted and swallowed two more pieces of pie.

'And . . . ONE!' Applejack shouted. 'Put the pies down, everypony!'

Applejack gave both Cranky and Mayor Mare an encouraging wink. Of all the ponies in Ponyville, she never thought it would be down to these two.

She and her friends Princess Twilight Sparkle, Fluttershy, Pinkie Pie, Rainbow Dash, and Rarity had all thought one of the big stallions in town would win. But Big McIntosh, Senior Mint, Overhaul, and Snowflake had all decided to sit it out this year to give somepony else a chance.

'The winner of the Sweet Apple Acres Pie-Eatin' Extravaganza is . . .' Applejack stepped forward on the wooden platform stage. 'Cranky Doodle Donkey!' The crowd erupted in cheers, and Mayor Mare nodded in approval at her competition. Apple Bloom placed a crown of apples on Cranky's head. He gave the filly a tiny smile, then immediately reverted to his trademark frown. Applejack turned to the crowd and held the megaphone up to her mouth. 'It sure was a close one, folks! Let's give all our pie eaters a round o' applause!'

The ponies stomped their hooves on the dirt and cheered. *It's real nice to see the underdog win,* thought Applejack. *Or, in this case, an underdonkey.* Either way, the pie-eating contest was much more exciting than in previous years. Applejack couldn't help but feel like it was one for the books.

'Is this over yet?' Cranky growled, ripping the crown off his prickly head. He was, after all, called 'Cranky' for a reason. 'I have things to do! I can't just hang around all day, you know.'

'Of course, champ,' Applejack smirked. She patted him on the back. 'Great job today.' He grunted and looked at her hoof as if he couldn't believe she'd touched him.

Matilda, his lady love, walked up to greet them. 'You won! I'm so proud,' she said with a smile. Applejack noticed a slight blush on Cranky's face.

'Enough with the compliments! I just ate some pie,' he grumbled.

'But you did it super-de-dooper awesomerifficaly!' Pinkie called out as she bounded over. She was still wearing her bib. She didn't look at all upset that she'd lost. 'You should be proud of yourself, too!'

'Way to go, Cranky!' said Twilight Sparkle as she, Rarity, Fluttershy, and

Rainbow Dash joined them.

Applejack could sense how uncomfortable Cranky was getting.

'All right, y'all. Give the champion his space.' She motioned for the ponies to step back. Cranky and Matilda nodded gratefully. As the two donkeys turned towards home, Applejack thought about how a pony never really knows what to expect from others. They sure could surprise ya!

Applejack had learned an important lesson today. And she didn't want to forget it. 'Heya, Twilight,' Applejack said. 'Who has our journal? I haven't written an entry in a long time, but I think I got somethin' to say about Cranky.'

Recently, the six ponies had been so tied up with other activities that they hadn't been writing in the journal they shared. Originally, they'd modelled it after the *Journal of the Two Sisters* that Princess Celestia and Princess Luna shared. But now it had become so much more than that to the friends. It was high time that one of them paid it a little attention. And that pony was going to be Applejack.

'Great idea!' Twilight grinned. She was always trying to get the others to participate in recording their lessons.

'Oh, I have it back at the boutique, darling,' Rarity said. 'I suppose the last thing I wrote about was my apprentice, Charity Sweetmint!'

'Whoo-ee! That pony sure was a hoof-ful.' Applejack nodded, recalling how the young fashionista had tried to become just like Rarity. 'But she sure meant well, of course.'

'Of course she did!' Rarity nodded, and her perfectly coiffed purple mane swayed gently. 'And you'll all be thrilled to hear that she's doing fabulously with her own line in Manehattan. She's being featured as a "Designer to Watch" in *PegasUs Weekly*!'

'That's great news! So I'll come on by and grab the journal now, if that's all right with you, Rarity,' Applejack said. 'Just got to clean up this mess, and I'll be right over.'

'I'll help!' Pinkie Pie squeaked. 'By taking some of those scrum-dillyumptious leftover pies off your hooves...' She patted her already bulging tummy. How she could eat any *more* pie after the contest was beyond Applejack. As Granny Smith would say, Pinkie Pie must have a 'hollow hoof' where she was hiding all that food!

'I think somepony already beat ya to it,' Applejack said. She pointed to the table. Apple Bloom and Sweetie Belle were already 'helping' by chowing down and making an even bigger mess. The six ponies all chuckled.

'Excuse me, ladies. I don't mean to interrupt,' said a beige-colored stallion with a light blue mane as he trotted up to the group. His cutie mark was a blue ribbon. A quick series of looks exchanged among the friends made it clear that nopony recognised him. 'But are you Applejack of Sweet Apple Acres?' he asked, raising an eyebrow.

'Yep, that's me.' Applejack tipped her hat. 'What can I do for ya?'

'My name is Blue Ribbon. I run the Best of Equestria Awards,' said the stallion. He passed Applejack a business card. Sure as the sun sits in the sky, it said:

Blue Ribbon

Best of Equestria Awards

Finding the Best Businesses in Equestria
Since the First Summer Sun Celebration

'I'm here to tell you that Sweet Apple

Acres has been named as a finalist in our Best Orchard in Equestria contest!'

'Really?' Applejack exclaimed.

'I mean, thank ya kindly, Mr Ribbon.' She looked to her friends, who had all started whispering excitedly to one another. 'Is there anything I need to do for ya?'

'Not too much . . .' Blue Ribbon smiled. He flipped open a folder filled with forms. He scanned the page with his hoof and jotted down some notes. 'We'll come by the farm on Friday to check out the place. If the harvest numbers you've reported to the *Equestria Farmers' Almanac* are correct, you've got nothing to worry about. That's some apple yield! I've never seen anything like it in all my years.'

'Well, we do try our best over at Sweet Apple Acres.' Applejack tried to recall the numbers they'd reported to the almanac. Applejack tipped her hat at Blue Ribbon. 'We'll be ready, sir.'

'I hope so,' Blue Ribbon said, putting his hoof on her shoulder. 'The winner of the award will be named the official apple supplier for Canterlot Castle.'

'How divine!' Rarity gasped. 'Does it include VIP access to all the events? For Applejack *and* her friends?'

'To the Wonderbolts Derby?!' said Rainbow Dash. 'Because that's the only one I really care about.'

Applejack shot her friends a look to shush them, but Rarity had a dreamy look in her eyes and Rainbow Dash had already stopped paying attention.

'There will be lots of special perks,' Blue Ribbon said. 'Front-row seats at the Equestria Rodeo definitely. Tickets to the

Hearth's Warming Eve Annual Ball. Oh, and one grand prize that is sure to delight any farmpony ...'

'That all sounds real nice, Mr Ribbon,' Applejack replied. 'But we Apples don't need any prizes—'

'What about a brand-new plot of land?' Blue Ribbon smirked.

Applejack's jaw dropped in surprise. Now that really *was* a prize worth winnin'!

Dear pony pal,
Here are some super exciting bonus pages just for you.
Why not share them with your friends too?
Love, Pinkie Pie

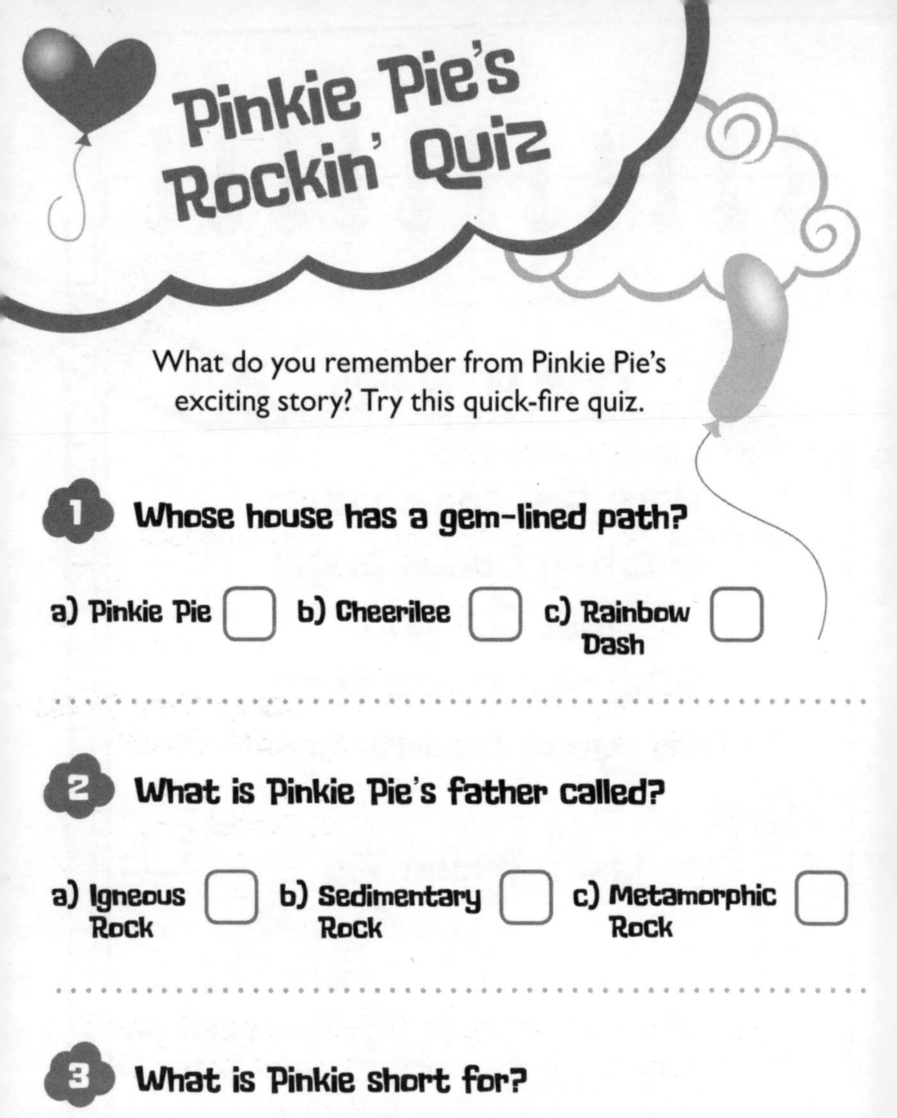

Pinkie Pie's Rockin' Quiz

What do you remember from Pinkie Pie's exciting story? Try this quick-fire quiz.

1 Whose house has a gem-lined path?

a) Pinkie Pie ☐ b) Cheerilee ☐ c) Rainbow Dash ☐

2 What is Pinkie Pie's father called?

a) Igneous Rock ☐ b) Sedimentary Rock ☐ c) Metamorphic Rock ☐

3 What is Pinkie short for?

a) Pinkleton ☐ b) Pinkles ☐ c) Pinkamena ☐

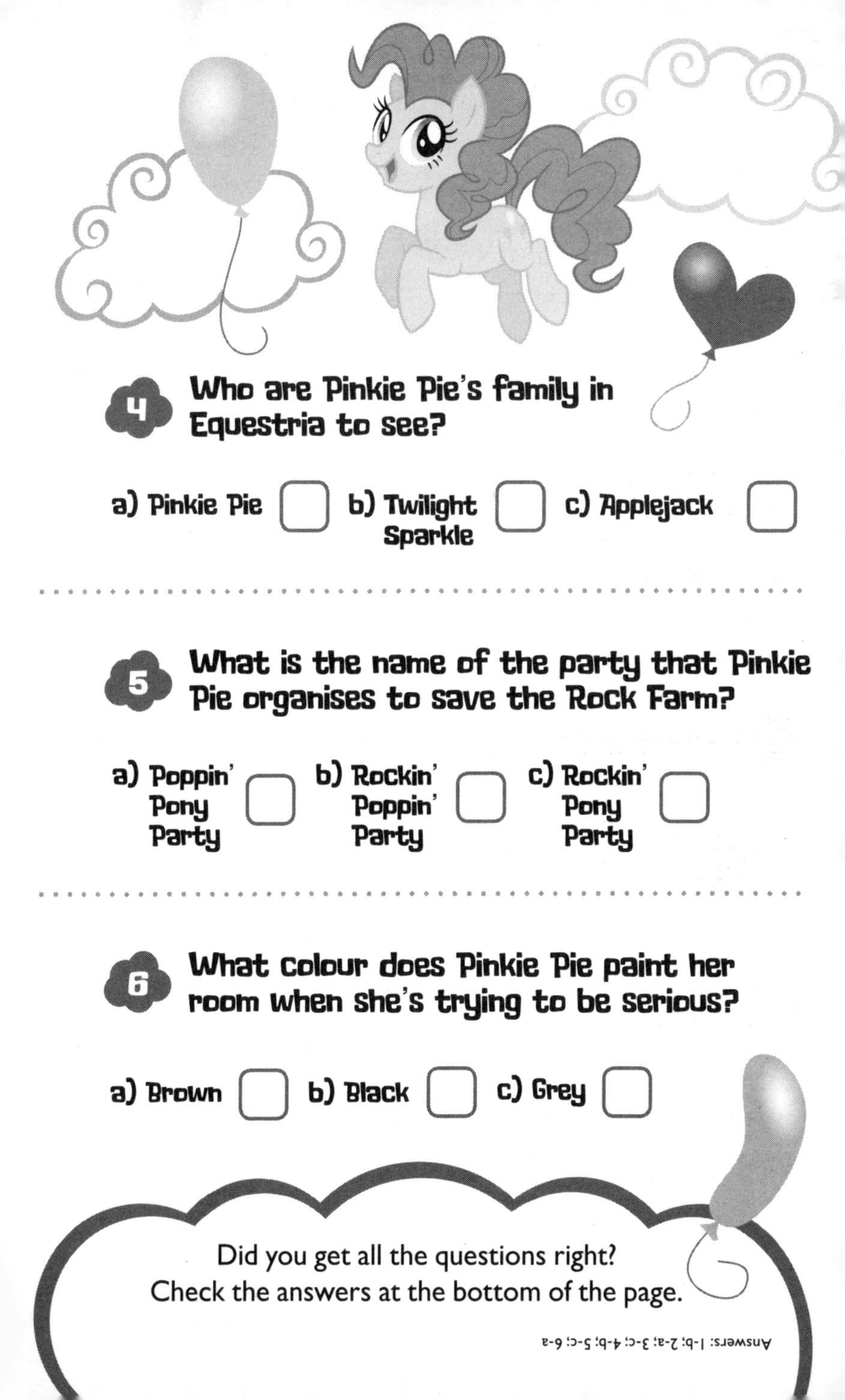

4 Who are Pinkie Pie's family in Equestria to see?

a) Pinkie Pie ☐ b) Twilight Sparkle ☐ c) Applejack ☐

5 What is the name of the party that Pinkie Pie organises to save the Rock Farm?

a) Poppin' Pony Party ☐ b) Rockin' Poppin' Party ☐ c) Rockin' Pony Party ☐

6 What colour does Pinkie Pie paint her room when she's trying to be serious?

a) Brown ☐ b) Black ☐ c) Grey ☐

Did you get all the questions right?
Check the answers at the bottom of the page.

Answers: 1-b; 2-a; 3-c; 4-b; 5-c; 6-a

Here's everything you need to know about Pinkie Pie!

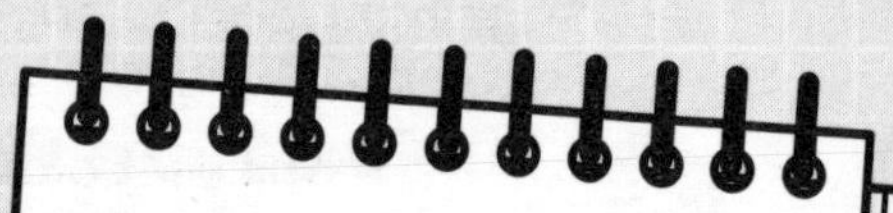

Species: Earth Pony

Element of Harmony: Laughter

Cutie Mark: Balloons

Likes: Parties

Dislikes: Being serious

Pet: Gummy

Pinkie Pie Dots
Join the dots to complete this picture of Pinkie Pie. When you've finished, why not colour it in too!

Elements of Harmony

Can you match the correct Element with the cutie mark of the pony who represents it? Draw lines between them, then check your answers at the bottom of the page.

Answers: 1-C; 2-A; 3-D; 4-B; 5-F; 6-E.

Ponyville Maze
Pinkie Pie has been playing with her Super Spring Sneakers and she has bounced right out of Ponyville! Can you help her find her way back to the town centre through the maze of paths?
START
FINISH
Answer:

Rockin' Wordsearch

Pinkie Pie is trying to remember all the different rocks. Can you help her find them? Words can be forwards, backwards or diagonally.

Q	G	J	L	G	R	A	N	I	T	E	M	R	U	Y
Q	H	S	E	A	B	T	O	D	N	Z	Y	S	F	W
A	E	T	A	L	S	W	M	O	R	O	Y	V	W	R
S	Q	E	Q	Q	P	H	T	A	I	E	Q	F	H	T
O	Q	N	S	L	L	S	R	H	R	G	H	Y	J	L
I	A	S	Z	B	E	R	M	L	V	B	O	I	F	A
Z	T	Q	T	M	V	A	A	I	E	O	L	N	U	S
M	L	Y	I	K	D	I	A	N	J	H	U	E	G	A
F	F	L	L	A	T	U	O	K	V	W	K	W	P	B
W	D	V	H	B	E	T	Y	H	T	T	N	L	F	A
T	Y	S	R	W	S	O	C	H	F	I	F	V	H	Y
H	R	J	V	D	F	S	H	J	V	C	H	T	T	Y
G	A	E	U	C	V	A	K	P	P	W	D	X	H	U
W	K	M	E	B	J	P	V	P	L	O	S	S	Q	S
X	F	U	N	W	J	A	T	W	Q	W	S	Q	D	S

SLATE
GRANITE
MARBLE
MUDSTONE
LIMESTONE
BASALT

Answer:

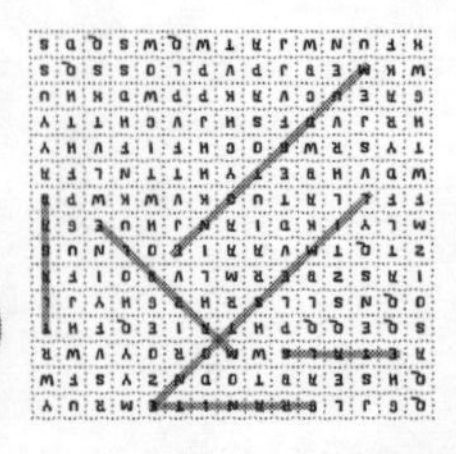

Party Planner

Pinkie just loves planning parties! If you were going to plan a party of your own, what kind of party would it be? Write about it below, using this guide to help you.

Is your party:

- Indoors?
- Outdoors?
- A surprise party?
- A costume party?

Add these fun words:

- Glitter
- Confetti
- Balloons
- Cupcakes

What's Your Pony Name?

Find out your pony name with this handy guide. Why not work out your friends' pony names too!

Take the first letter of your name:

- A - STRAWBERRY
- B - DAREDEVIL
- C - RAINBOW
- D - STARBURST
- E - VIOLET
- F - SUNSET
- G - TULIP
- H - REBEL
- I - LUNA
- J - POPPY
- K - RUBY
- L - FIRE
- M - PEACH
- N - FIERCE
- O - HAPPY
- P - SUNSHINE
- Q - BUTTERCUP
- R - DISCO
- S - DANDELION
- T - FUZZY
- U - FLASH
- V - TWINKLE
- W - GIDDY
- X - DAYDREAM
- Y - BUBBLE
- Z - PRANCING

And the month you were born:

January - MOON
February - MANE
March - FLASH
April - BLOSSOM
May - SPRINKLES
June - TAIL
July - PHOENIX
August - WINGS
September - CLOUD
October - BEAM
November - SNOWFLAKE
December - GLITTER

My pony name is:

....

Your Pony

Species:

Cutie Mark:

Likes:

Dislikes:

Pet:

Now you know your pony name, it's time to create your very own pony character. Decorate and colour in the pony on the page, and fill in your own pony profile. Are you a Pegasus, a Unicorn or even an Alicorn? It's up to you!

Pinkie Puzzle

Can you find the picture of Pinkie that's different from the others?

Did you solve the puzzle?
Check your answer at the bottom of the page.

Answer: C is the odd one out.

Fun with Friends

Pinkie Pie loves to spend time with her friends. Here are some ideas for things you can do with yours.

Write your own short story together!

You'll need at least one friend. Simply get a blank piece of paper and start writing the first sentence. When you've finished, pass it on to a friend and when they've finished they pass it back to you or to another friend. Soon you'll have written your own Daring Do mystery!

Throw your very own tea party!

You'll need some friends to come over. Oh, and some tea and cakes too!

Comedy show!

Why not put on a comedy show with your friends? Everyone can tell their favourite jokes and funny stories.

Nature Trail!

Next time you're outside with your friends, why not jot down what plants, birds and animals you spot. You'll notice nature is everywhere!

Home Sweet Home

It's time for Pinkie Pie to get back to Sugarcube Corner. But only one of these paths leads there. Can you show her the way?

Answer: Path C

Congratulations on completing all these extra special puzzle pages. Pinkie Pie is off to plan another party!
See you soon!

Discover more magical MY LITTLE PONY books!

EGMONT